MAMA REX AND T
Lose a Waffle

by Rachel Vail
illustrations by Steve Björkman

SCHOLASTIC INC.
New York Toronto London Auckland Sydney
Mexico City New Delhi Hong Kong

To Zachary,
who fell in a puddle
and lost a waffle
but found a story

ISBN 0-439-19918-2

Text copyright © 2000 by Rachel Vail.
Art copyright © 2000 Steve Bjorkman.

12 11 10 9 8 7 6 5 4   1 2 3 4 5 6/0

Book Design by Cristina Costantino

Printed in the U.S.A.
First Scholastic printing, October 2000

Contents

Chapter 1
A NICE, CALM MORNING

Mama Rex and T had to leave by 8:15.
It was already 8:16.

"I don't think we're going to make it," T said.

"We ARE going to make it," Mama Rex said
from inside her sweater. "We have to. We can't be
late again."

She gulped coffee from her favorite mug—the
one T had made for her—as she finished ironing
her skirt on the table.

T sat down on his special chair to think. After a minute, T said, "Let's talk about time."

Mama Rex was under the table. She was gathering her papers and finding one shoe but not the other.

"Can time ever move backward?" T asked. "Like, can time subtract?"

"Go brush your teeth," Mama Rex answered.

T meant to go straight to the bathroom, but the rain pounding on the window distracted him.

"T!" Mama Rex yelled, and he remembered.

"I wish I didn't have so many teeth," T mumbled through toothpaste bubbles.

"Cereal or a waffle?" Mama Rex called to T.

"Waffle," T answered, spitting out the tooth-paste. "Are these clean enough?"

"Blue or white?" Mama Rex asked.

T looked into the sink. "Bluish-white," he answered. "More toward white."

"Good enough!" Mama Rex said.

T heard a crash in the kitchen. "Ack!" yelled Mama Rex. "Quick, quick! Let's go!"

T chose a jacket from his coatrack. He picked his yellow raincoat. There were two leaves in the pocket. T had collected them.

"T!" Mama Rex yelled.

T hurried.

Mama Rex shoved a warm waffle into T's mouth and the big blue lunch box into T's backpack.

T wiggled his shoulders into his backpack straps.

Mama Rex grabbed her umbrella and T's from the closet.

"Hooray!" said T. T loved his umbrella. Anywhere he went with it, he had his own clubhouse hideaway. Under his umbrella, T always felt safe and powerful.

T wished he could open his umbrella right away, or at least whack the couch with it to hear what sound it would make, but he knew better.

Mama Rex sloshed more coffee into her mug, bit her key ring with her teeth, draped her briefcase over her shoulder, opened the door, and held it with her foot.

T took the waffle out of his mouth and saw the semicircle his bite had made. His waffle looked like a boat. T imagined it bobbing along on the ocean.

"OK, T," said Mama Rex. "We're out of here."

Mama Rex and T looked at the clock.
The clock said 8:21.

Mama Rex unplugged the clock.

"I think we might still make it," said Mama Rex.

She grabbed T's free hand. It fit perfectly
in hers.

"I think so, too," said T.

Chapter 2
OUT IN THE STORM

The elevator was very slow.

Mama Rex pushed the DOWN button six times.

On the way down, T counted the floor numbers by odds.

T asked, "Why isn't there a thirteenth floor?"

"I have a meeting at nine," Mama Rex said.

"Nine is an odd number," said T.

"Very," said Mama Rex.

Mama Rex and T ran across the lobby.

Mama Rex held her umbrella under her arm so she could yank T's hood over his large head.

T didn't like his hood. "I have an umbrella," he told her.

"I don't want you to get soaked," Mama Rex said, and they went through the revolving door out into the storm.

In the courtyard outside their building,
there was a little puddle.
T stomped in it.
It made a terrific splash.

"T!" yelled Mama Rex. "Now your feet will be wet all day."

T smiled at Mama Rex.

"That's OK," said T. "It was fun."

Mama Rex smiled, too, a smaller smile than T's.

At the corner, T watched the DON'T WALK sign.
The red letters were blurry behind the rain.
T tilted his head to get a drink of rain, but above him was a ceiling of umbrellas.
The grown-ups under the umbrellas were making stomachache faces.

DON'T WALK changed to WALK.

T put his waffle in his mouth so he could hold
Mama Rex's hand to cross the street.

When T stepped off the sidewalk, there was no
street under his foot.

There was a puddle, and under the puddle was
more puddle.

Down, down, down went T, into the puddle. His shoes were wet, then his pants were wet, and his jacket, all the way up to his armpits.

Mama Rex dropped her briefcase and her mug and her umbrella. What she didn't drop was T's hand. She yanked that hand up, and with the hand came the rest of T, up and out of the puddle.

The grown-ups under the umbrellas picked up Mama Rex's things while Mama Rex hugged T.

T was trying not to cry.

"Waffle!" T yelled.

"I know, sweetheart," said Mama Rex, kissing T all over. "It's awful. That was scary and awful. Are you hurt?"

The grown-ups under the umbrellas all leaned forward.

"No!" yelled T. "Not 'awful.' Waffle!"

"What?" asked Mama Rex.

T held his waffle high in the rain. It looked terrible. The waffle had fallen out of his mouth and into the puddle.

T had found it, but now the waffle had clumps of mud and dry leaves stuck to it, and it was grayish-wet.

As T was showing his waffle to Mama Rex, the bottom half dripped off, *gunk*, down to the sidewalk.

"Waffle!" cried T.

Mama Rex smiled. "A waffle," said Mama Rex, "is not a good thing to take puddle-jumping."

T smiled, a smaller smile than Mama Rex's.

The grown-ups under the umbrellas crossed the street.

Mama Rex and T stayed on the corner. Mama Rex gathered up their wet things.

"I'm pretty sure there's another waffle in the freezer," she said, and tossed the rest of the soggy one into a garbage can on their way back home.

T's feet kept moving but his eyes stayed on the garbage can.

"Waffle," he said again sadly.

In their courtyard, Mama Rex stomped in the little puddle.

"Hmm," she said to T. "You were right."

Chapter 3
THE LAST WAFFLE

Mama Rex helped T pull off his wet clothes.
They hung everything from the shower rod.
Now it was raining inside, too.

T put on dry socks while Mama Rex looked for a new waffle in the freezer.

"Is there one?" T asked.

"You're in luck!" Mama Rex yelled back. "There's one last waffle!"

T sat down on his bed.

"Are you dressed?" Mama Rex asked from the kitchen.

"Almost," said T, standing up. He went to his dresser to find fresh clothes.

"Let's see who will win—you or the toaster," suggested Mama Rex.

T hurried. He wanted to beat the toaster.

T was halfway into his shirt when the toaster dinged.

"Tie!" said Mama Rex.

T chose his other jacket.

Mama Rex changed her shoes and picked up her briefcase and umbrella.

T took the waffle from her and held his umbrella in the other hand.

Mama Rex opened the door.

"Mama Rex?" asked T.

"Yes?" She leaned against the door frame.

"This is the last waffle?" T asked.

"Yes," said Mama Rex.

"Oh, no," said T. "What will we do if I fall into the puddle again?"

Mama Rex stepped back into their home and closed the door.

She looked at the unplugged clock. It said nothing.

Mama Rex put down her briefcase and umbrella and unbuttoned her jacket.

"Come on," she said to T.

T followed Mama Rex to the kitchen.

Mama Rex put T's waffle on a plate and poured some syrup on top.

She took her favorite mug—the one T had made for her—out of the sink and filled it with coffee.

Mama Rex and T went to the living room.

While Mama Rex spread out her papers on the table and talked on the phone with her office, T ate his waffle with a fork.

He imagined each bite falling into the syrup puddle and getting wet and sticky.

After they were done, Mama Rex and T sat in their chairs the rest of the morning, watching the rain and talking about time.